To Melissa
from Nanny

To Melissa
from Nanny

MATTIE
— AND —
CATARAGUS

MATTIE
— AND —
CATARAGUS
by Dennis Kyte

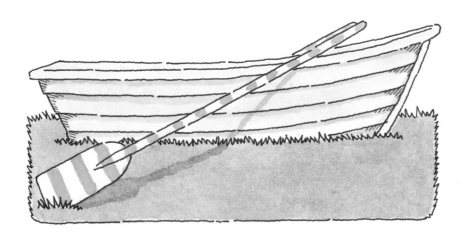

Doubleday
New York

Text and illustrations © 1988 by Dennis Kyte
All rights reserved
First Edition
Printed in the United States of America

Library of Congress Cataloging-in-Publication Data

Kyte Dennis, 1947–
Mattie and Cataragus/by Dennis Kyte.—1st ed.
p.   cm.
Summary: Cataragus, a quiet and shy gentleman cat, finds his life
turned upside down when he becomes infatuated with the lovely Mattie
and goes to enormous lengths to have her notice him.
ISBN 0-385-24403-7   ISBN 0-385-24404-5 (lib. bdg.)
[1. Cats—Fiction.]   I. Title.
PZ7.K993Mat 1988   87-23588
[E]—dc19   CIP
                                                                        AC

In the heart, it is always Spring.

Cataragus was a shy gentleman cat who lived in the cottage that was on the path that crossed the hill that led to the market town of Peas-Blossom.

He lived alone, but his quiet, peaceful life was about to change.

One summer morning a lovely lady cat named Mattie appeared
at the bottom of the hill just outside the green tunnel of elms
that led from the forest to the market town of Peas-Blossom.
    She walked to market on the path that crossed the
hill that passed the house of Cataragus.

From his window, Cataragus saw Mattie as she paused for a moment to fuss and fiddle with her basket and bows. "OH, GREAT CATS!" he whispered to himself. "How ever shall I meet her?"

After he had watched her for weeks, it became clear that every Saturday Mattie went to the market to buy fishtails and dandelions for stew. Cataragus practiced what to say to her, but every Saturday when Mattie walked by he said nothing. He was just too shy.

One Saturday morning he finally worked up his courage. "Today I do it," he thought. "I say 'Good morning, what a lovely day.'" As Mattie approached he stepped out and said in his boldest kitty voice, "Bry, mug gurning...lov a woodly...OH NO!...What have I said? OH, GREAT CATS!"

and with that he fainted and keeled right over into his lilies.

Mattie stopped and looked around to see who had spoken to her. But, seeing no one, she simply adjusted her hat, smoothed her dress, and continued on her way down the path to the market town of Peas-Blossom.

Cataragus was so embarrassed that he wouldn't come out of his house for two days. But, while tidying up his closet, he found some gray felt that had been lying around for ages. "This gives me an idea!" Cataragus thought, giggling. The next Saturday, as the leaves were turning red and gold, he leaped out of the bushes, dressed up as a giant mouse, and offered Mattie a gooey piece of cheese.

Mattie simply patted the unknown mouse on its gray felt nose. "Silly, silly, silly," she said, and continued on her way to market. Cataragus started to run after her, but he tripped over his mouse tail and fell splat on his face. "OH, GREAT CATS!" muttered the mouse, now covered with gooey cheese.

The Saturday after that, Cataragus got himself a great big red balloon. "Oh, she will like this," he said to himself as he puffed and puffed and puffed in the last bit of air. But he forgot to tie the end.

Just as he presented it, the balloon took off with Cataragus still hanging on to it, sputtering and phumphering, around and around the lawn, clear up into the clouds and out of sight. "Silly, silly, silly," said Mattie as she continued to town.

Then one frosty morning Cataragus made a wonderful wooden wagon and, with shiny purple paint, printed "MATTIE" on the sides. "Oh, she will like this," he said to himself as he put the finishing touches on the wagon. It had big red wheels and a shiny ribbon tied around its handle. But as Mattie neared, Cataragus was so nervous…that he fell over backward into the wagon, which raced down the hill, passed Mattie, crashed into a tree, and broke into a hundred tiny little pieces. Lying under the tree, Cataragus heard very faintly "Silly, silly, silly," as Mattie disappeared over the hill.

Winter kept Cataragus indoors, where he practiced a serenade on his tuba. "Oh, she will like this song," he said as he put on his muffler and went outside. He stood ready, and when Mattie approached took a deep breath and played as loud as he could.

He played so loud that he caused an avalanche to fall from his snow-covered roof. Rumble, rumble, SPLAT! A snow-covered Cataragus heard "Silly, silly, silly," as Mattie slogged through the snow on her way to market.

Spring arrived and with it new ideas to win Mattie's friendship. "Oh, Mattie likes flowers, I know that," Cataragus said to himself. He hummed as he watered his garden. The flowers were so tall that Cataragus could not see over them. "She will be so surprised!" he muttered happily.

And Mattie *was* surprised. She thought she had fallen victim to a sudden cloudburst. It was not until she cleaned the mud from her dress that she heard Cataragus humming. Marching away on the muddy path, she cried "This is NOT silly, silly, silly! This is just plain rude!" Cataragus covered his eyes and groaned, "OH, GREAT CATS!"

The next morning that Mattie went to market, she put on her roller skates. "Enough of this silliness," Mattie said to herself, "I am *too* smart and *too* fast for any surprises today!"

Suddenly, she stopped and looked ahead of her, not believing her eyes. Cataragus was putting the finishing touches on a great big bridge made of stones.

"A bridge…here in the middle of a meadow?" Mattie asked herself. "This is too silly!" and decided to tell him so. And so she did.

Cataragus turned around, startled to see Mattie standing right there in front of him... close enough for him to notice she smelled of lavender. He smiled, but his smile quickly faded. "Well, Mr. Cataragus," Mattie began, "you have done many silly things, to be sure, but this is the silliest! You are building a bridge where there is no river for hundreds of miles. A bridge is for crossing a river... a river, Mr. Cataragus! Why? Why would you do something so silly?

And what's this?"

Mattie saw an envelope on the bridge. The envelope had her
name on it. "OH, mail for me!" she said. She took the envelope
and tucked it in her basket, turned, and walked down the path to
the market town of Peas-Blossom. Cataragus could hear her saying
"Silly, silly, silly" all the way down the path. He lowered his eyes,
and a tiny tear fell to the ground.

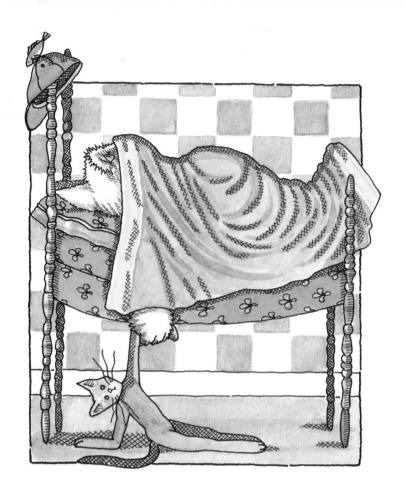

Cataragus was devastated. Slowly he walked up the hill to his cottage, went inside, locked the door and pulled down the shades, and sadly went to bed that night without supper.

That same evening Mattie returned home to her cottage. Her market basket was full of the day's treasures. She put everything away and at the bottom of the basket she saw the envelope. It made her think of Cataragus and she muttered again, "Silly, silly, silly" as she opened it. Inside was the sweetest, silliest poem.

IF YOU WERE MY FRIEND
by CATARAGUS

I would bring you a sandwich
    Of moonbeams on toast.
A jar full of colors,
    the ones you like most.

An ice cream bird
    Would sit in a dish
It would sing out your name
    And you'd make a wish

The wish would come true
    The stars would all shine
Because I would be your friend
    And you would be mine.

The next morning Cataragus felt awful. He was humiliated and sick at heart. "She's right," he said to himself. "I am silly and the first thing I will do is tear down that silly bridge." Cataragus got out of bed and opened the door. The sky was bright and clear. The sun was shining on his bridge. He shaded his eyes and squinted. "OH, GREAT CATS!" he exclaimed, for there under the bridge and in the tall grass was a beautiful blue rowboat.

He ran down the hill as fast as he could. There was someone in the boat. As she lowered her parasol, he saw that it was Mattie. She looked at Cataragus and smiled and purred…"Care to join me for a picnic on the river, Mr. Cataragus?"

"Well, GREAT CATS!" he said as he kicked off his boots, rolled up his trousers, and waded through the grass toward the blue rowboat and his new friend.

And Mattie and Cataragus spent the day together
fishing for butterflies.